To my dear, Maciee!
Love that you look
looks like your Aunt Amon!

Dream Big!
Neigh ann

to My Moon
Bound Girl,

_____

from
_____

with love to the moon and back

In Memory

of my beloved brother, Tony Leonard,
who dreamed in music, too.

~la

ISBN 978-1-7331023-8-4

Author and Illustrator: Leigh Ann Agee

Request for rights and permissions, please contact:
Moon Bound Girl
P.O Box 683
Bristol, TN 37621-0683
www.moonboundgirl.com

Publishing services provided by Fitting Words. www.fittingwords.net

Graphic art services provided by LACreative.

Distributed by APG Sales. www.apg-sales.com

Printed in China

My name is **Harmony**
And I am bound for the *Moon!*

I knew it the night I looked to the sky
And belted out my very first tune!

I had no idea if my voice
sounded beautiful
Or if anyone would want to hear it

All I knew was that each note I sang
filled my *heart,*
soul and
spirit

The moon witnessed the moment
The first song left my lips
And gave me a fluttering butterfly feeling
That made my hair magically lift

It *swirled* and *floated*
toward the moon
Til each strand twirled around

I knew I was shooting for the moon
With this passion I had found

I sent up a wish and held my breath
And like magic, the stars aligned

As I sang myself to sleep that night
wonderful visions flooded my mind

A music staff rolled out like a highway

Completely circling the globe

As I tossed and turned in my covers

I went everywhere I could dream of to go.

It was a starry night in Paris

Where my dream was destined to begin

As I strummed my guitar on the Eiffel Tower

I could hear

Mona Lisa join in!

With a wink I was suddenly in Ireland

Playing fiddle for some dancing sheep

The flock blocked the street behind me

while I sang to a truck's

Beep Beep.

With a snore

I went to Holland

And rode a bicycle

built for two

Singing duets with

the waving tulips

While pedaling in

wooden shoes.

With a sleepy sigh

I climbed on a camel

In Egypt, that's like a car

I rode through the streets in Cairo

Singing solo while playing sitar.

I rode a majestic Chinese dragon

In the Lunar New Year's parade

While dressed in colorful silk qipaos

Dancers moved to the

songs I played.

I joined a chorus in England

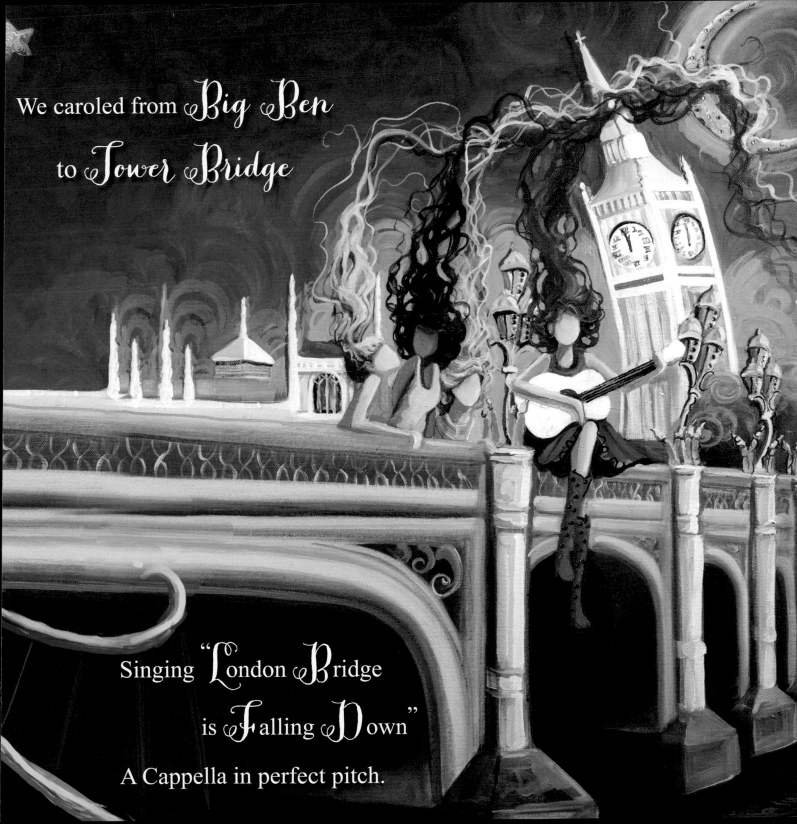

We caroled from *Big Ben*
to *Tower Bridge*

Singing "*London Bridge*
is *Falling Down*"

A Cappella in perfect pitch.

I rolled over and was in Kenya

With a giraffe singing

campfire songs

While lions, tigers

and zebras (*oh my*)

and even the elephants

sang along.

With a sigh

I was in Nashville

I saw why its called Music City

Even the buildings danced and swayed

To every beat of my little ditty.

The moon in Mexico was

bright as a marigold

illuminating sugar skulls in yellow and red

As we honored the spirits of loved ones

In celebration of the

Day of the Dead.

I sang opera

from a bridge in Venice

Where the canals are

the same as streets

And serenaded

Moonstruck

sweethearts

In gondolas

sailing beneath.

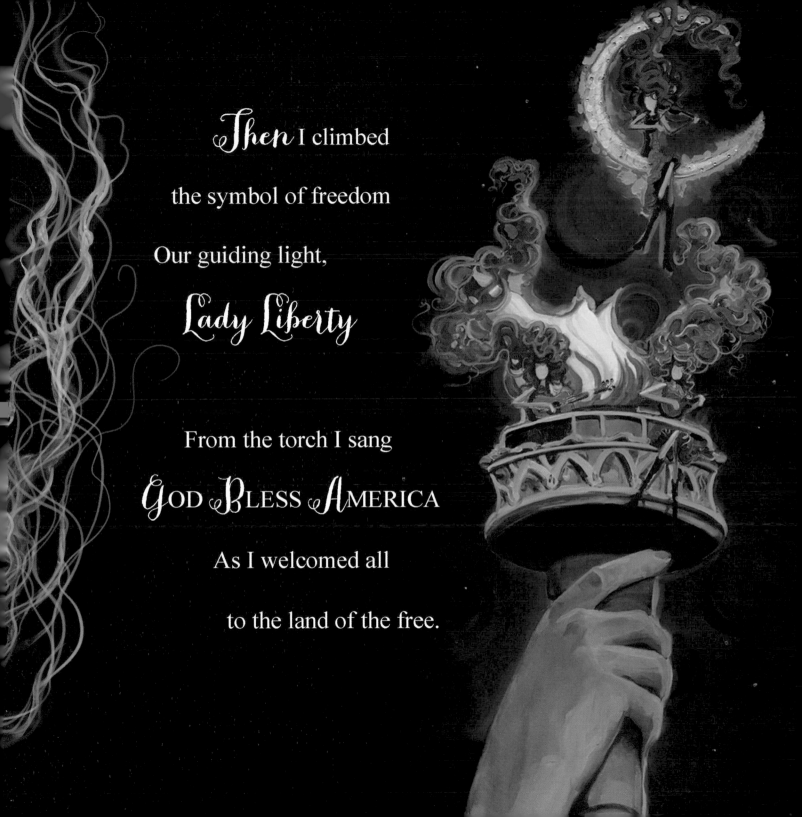

Then I climbed

the symbol of freedom

Our guiding light,

Lady Liberty

From the torch I sang

God Bless America

As I welcomed all

to the land of the free.

I saw passion across the planet

Hopes and dreams in a million faces

Of passionate dreamers all over the world

Shooting for the moon

in all its phases.

So wherever on earth you are

The same moon shines above

Offering in all the universal languages

Passion,

Art,

Music

and *Love*

We Moon Bound Girls

can follow our hearts

With each and every step

The Closer we get to reaching

our dreams

We'll keep asking....

Are We There Yet?

You are a
Moon
Bound Girl too!

What do you love to do more than anything else? _____

_____

_____

_____

_____

_____

_____

How can you shoot for the moon with your passion? _____

_____

_____

What are three things you can do to move your dream closer to your goals? _____

_____

_____

_____

_____

Where in the world will your *dreams* lead you?

You'll find out if you follow your *Heart!*

Believing in your *Joy* and *Passion*

Is the Perfect Place to start!

Harmony

Moon
Bound
Girl

www.moonboundgirl.com

Hey, you just gotta

keep dreamin'…